We Are Together

by Britta Teckentrup

To Ian
~ Britta

tiger tales

On our own, we're special,
and we can chase our dream.
But when we join up, hand in hand,
together, we're a team.

We may travel alone,
free as birds in the sky,
but by flocking together,
we soar and we fly.

If storm clouds gather,
and we're caught in the rain,
let's splash through the puddles
till the sun shines again.

We can change the world
with the power of words.
We can all join together,
to let our voices be heard!

Hear the song we sing
to encourage and inspire.

If we all sing together,
one voice becomes a choir.

Walking all together,
on paths as yet unknown,
may lead us to places
that feel just like home.

We're off to climb mountains,
all the way to the top.

Our friends keep us going—
they won't let us stop.

Embrace all life's colors—
each shade, every hue—

and life will be brighter
whenever you do.

When the icy wind blows
and winter takes hold,

your friends keep you warm,
so you won't feel the cold.

When life is confusing,
and our way seems unclear,
the horizon is distant,
but our friends will stay near.

At the end of each day
as we watch the night fall,
a million bright stars
shine down on us all.

If ever we're lonely,
we'll just say out loud:
let's all stand together,
one big, happy crowd!